Freedom

Play Championship World-Class Tennis with Bjorn McEnroe

Sean::Adrian::Brijbasi

Published simultaneously in the United
States and Great Britain in 2018
by Pretend Genius
Copyright © Sean::Adrian::Brijbasi

ISBN: 978-0-9995277-4-0

other books by Sean::Adrian::Brijbasi

One Note Symphonies
for Emma

Still Life in Motion
for those who play
Marius and Andréus

The Unknowed Things
for Julius

The Dictionary of Coincidences, Volume i
for Emma

S{E}AN?
for EM{M}A+

E{M}MA+ the ghost orchids
for Emma

darling two hearts
for E{M}MA+ the ghost orchids

Stories for Nadira
for Adrian, Andréus, Elijah, Helena, Julius,
Marius, Nadira

for
Adrian
Andréus
Elijah
Helena
Julius
Marius
Nadira

the tennis contents

the tennis lob

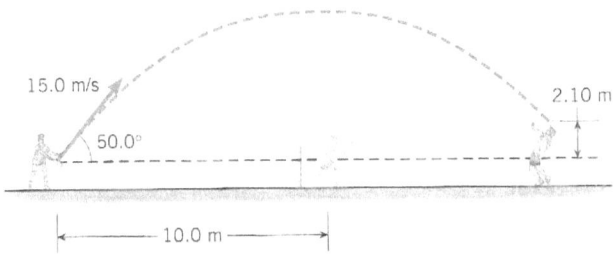

It came from my blood though not from my blood alone. It was everything that I had ever seen and forgotten that had come to be dissolved in my blood. The sadness at seeing those we love suffer the small disappointments they no longer remembered, the overlooked pleasure of the unexpected hours we spent cleaning our garden and drinking tea between late afternoon rain storms, the unseen tears you cried for your father, for your mother, for your children, and for me, while I slept beside you, the dream I had that in the morning I would not remember but nevertheless do remember and will always remember in the universe of dreams.

Everything was in my blood and I watched it spill out from my face like barely remembered black-and-white cinema film after being hit by a tennis ball travelling hundreds (perhaps thousands) of miles an hour.

The observed cause: Lelolah distracted me as she walked across the parking lot behind the chain link fence that separated the tennis court from the rest of the world at the very moment that my partner hit a lob to the other side of the net. I remember seeing the ball take its upward arc, reach its pinnacle, my eyes closing, my eyes opening, then my face and shirt wet with blood (my nose had been brutally struck).

Conjecture as to the primary unobserved cause: there were particular moments while I played tennis on that otherwise uneventful day that my mind wandered. Once to the sun which reminded me—and speaking of the sun, it was as if the tennis ball was a wayward asteroid that hit a planet and caused massive destruction that spewed debris into the cold, dark universe (a more apt simile than "like barely remembered black-and-white cinema film")—but the sun reminded me of a time when I thought about how far away you were and of how our lives might intersect if we both looked at the sun at the same time.

Another time to the essence of the lob after I returned the spin serve of my friend (DJ Titan T-Rex) cross-court and away from his girlfriend (Margaret) at the net. She reached to her right but the ball sizzled past her and while it did I hurried to the net in anticipation of the point-winning volley. It was during this time (the time between me returning serve and running to the net) that my mind wandered to the essence of the lob.

I had no conclusions as to the essence of the lob or, if I did, the tennis ball that struck me so brutally knocked the memory of those conclusions right out of my head. But if I were to think of it now then I would say that the essence of the lob is despair. It could be something else.

haiku 1

[top boy]

standing on the roof
top boy waves to his ma-
ma yells I love you

untranslated

Dear darling,

After your WICKED
ways I've decided to
stay at your
parents' house for a
few days so I can
draw some pictures
for your book.
Your parents have

the tennis racquet

I think about the natural substances like wood and grass which reminds me that my first tennis racquet was made out of wood and the first tennis match I saw was played on grass.

The tennis racquet was a gift from my uncle (who I could never imagine playing tennis but who, nevertheless, did). There was a small crack in the racquet frame so that if the ball didn't hit the center of the racquet strings it felt as though the racquet would bend backwards (perhaps the number one reason that I never mishit a tennis ball).

But the racquet was sturdy enough for me to hit tennis balls against the brick wall of the nearby elementary school.

"This forever taught me a lesson about the usefulness of cracked objects."

--Bjorn McEnroe

The first un-cracked object I used as a tennis racquet with which to hit a tennis ball was a book—a flat, thin book, perhaps one of those coffee table books that were *a la mode* at the end of the last century.

As part of my human development my parents took me to a party at their friend's house and in the basement of the house I found a tennis ball. "In the beginning" I bounced the ball against the wall with my hand (possibly both hands). My goal was to never drop the ball after it bounced back to me but I did drop it and when I went to retrieve it from the narrow mouth between the sofa and the floor I saw the book near where a sofa epiglottis might be. I reached in with my entire arm and carefully pulled the book out. I spent most of the night hitting the tennis ball against the wall with the book until we left the party.

I did stop twice—once to eat and another time when I heard people arguing upstairs (just before we "vamoosed"). It sounded like someone had shown up to the party uninvited and I could hear my father telling his friend to let her stay but his friend said that she caused trouble the last time and was always causing trouble and didn't want her to stay. I didn't hear my mother's voice. I imagined that she was whispering in my father's ear while he spoke.

I climbed to the top of the stairs using my hands and feet (something I still do as a form of exercise) and sat down on the third step from the top.   I pushed the door open just enough for me to see into the kitchen. I didn't see my mother or father but I saw other people—one of them a woman I had never seen before. I couldn't see her face but I saw her legs.

I wouldn't have been able to describe then the feeling I had when I saw her legs. But if I think back on it now I would say that her legs were beautiful even though I may not have known what it meant for legs to be beautiful. Perhaps I could only reflect on them as objects, which in the eyes of some people "ain't cool", but I didn't know the potential of legs and I was too young to understand the feeling that overcame me.

When we went home later that night I remember my mother and father holding hands in the old car that my mother drove to take us from here to there (pretty much anywhere) and back. I sat quietly in the seat behind my father and stared at their hands until the entanglement of their fingers looked like something alien to me. I thought I could think that way about legs too if I looked at them long enough.

drawn on all the photographs they have of you. On some they've drawn long hair and on others they've drawn long eye lashes (or both), which makes you look pretty but also makes me feel a bit

haiku 2

[rain children]

walking past green fields
dried by sunlight after
rain children play

translated from ima-apano

[cthiti i-a-pa]

omsili i-a-ma gra
so-si-a-sa
tok cthiti i-a-pa

sorry for you even though I shouldn't because you should suffer a little bit for what you've done. I still LOVE (love love) you but maybe being here is a small destiny because when I look at the photographs

the tennis footwork

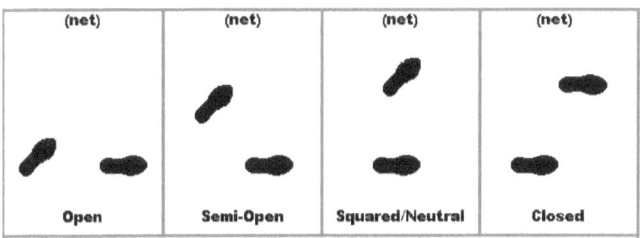

(net)	(net)	(net)	(net)
Open	Semi-Open	Squared/Neutral	Closed

I'd often thought about asking my parents about the party that was so essential to my human development. I had it in my mind to leave the comfort of the tennis court and go find the book that started my foray into championship world-class tennis playing.

I imagined that I would go on TV or radio shows and hold the book up and say "kids, this is what started it all for me, a book, books are important" or something similar. Maybe "books are the key to success" or "you can't be successful without a book". I had time to think about it. I could also make my book statement palatable for adults.

Finding the book could be easy: ask my parents for the names of the people who had the party we went to that night, ask those people about the book I found underneath the sofa in their basement, and then go get the book from them. Everything could line up perfectly and I would know everything there was to know about getting the book in less than an hour and possibly get the book within a day or two depending on where those people lived.

I haven't asked my parents about the party, however, because I've been preoccupied by my championship world-class tennis career. I compared (in my mind) finding the book that set me on the path of my life to using tennis footwork. I was so dedicated to being the best in the world that

I used the most common daily doings as fodder for my practice and preparation to be the best in the world ever (not just the best in the world at that time).

I thought (again in my own mind) that it would take three steps to get the book. It's the same in tennis—efficiency of movement is the key to great victories (remember the Great Combined Ethiopian Open in 1998 that I won in five sets against then number one player John Borg). Sometimes I had to take little footsteps to victory but those little footsteps were adjustments at the point of contact with the ball when the wind or invisible moisture affected the movement of the ball so that all the predictions I made as to the speed and final position of the ball were skewed by unseen outside forces I had not (and humanly could not) take into account.

I wouldn't take little footsteps to get the book until: 1) I found the people who had the party, 2) they said they had the book, 3) they said they would give me the book but, 4) when I finally met them in person they changed their minds and wanted to keep the book instead.

That's when those little footsteps to make adjustments at the point of contact with the ball are important in order to hit the ball perfectly or in this case: get the book.

"Take little footsteps in the world."

--Bjorn McEnroe

haiku 3

[spring]

making tea in her garden
she stirs passing clouds

translated from khavo

[umsisani]

inmimiti drinastas
mimidrit staaki

that your parents
drew on I feel
inspired so I think
this is where I am
supposed to be at
this particular time
in the still and
seemingly ever-
flow(er)ing
universe. They
drew on them with

the tennis drop shot

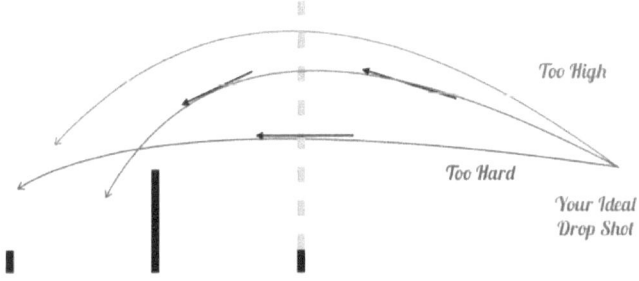

It's fascinating to me that when I'm sleeping there are billions of other humans who are also sleeping. Some, perhaps hundreds of millions, lie down at the exact same moment that I lie down. Others, perhaps millions, fall asleep at the exact same moment that I fall asleep.

There is also the matter of waking which comes with its own inexplicable statistics or sleeping itself and the hundreds of thousands of humans who turn to their left or to their right at the exact same moment that I turn to my left or to my right in some kind of strange cosmic choreography.

Sometimes before I fall asleep I think about the trees or bushes or flowers I had seen throughout the day being blown "to and fro" by the wind. I might remember a tree or bush or flower from a previous day but I try to remember a tree or bush or flower from the same day.

I remember how the wind bends the stalks of the flowers or the limbs of the trees—bends them in one direction and then another. The wind blows over everything in its path (flowers, bushes, trees, and even humans) as if it were singing tributes to the dying or the already dead.

"Who sings tributes to the wind which seems never-ending but will (surely?) end one day?"

--Bjorn McEnroe

Everyone who watches championship world-class tennis knows that I don't play my best tennis in windy conditions (remember the match I won against Steffi Navratilova in which I barely avoided what would have been the second greatest upset of tennis history—the first being the time that I, as an unknown tennis player, beat then number one player Goodnight Obi-Johnson-Smith of New Zealand).

One of the most important things to remember is to never try a drop shot during windy conditions unless you are a championship world-class tennis player. A well-executed drop shot is like a kiss of soft devastation (a.k.a. plush ruin).

In the spirit of the wind and tributes—a drop shot is a fleeting homage to the opponent on the other side of the net who may dig deep within their soul to hit another shot but who will ultimately fail.

Just memorize this formula for drop shot success: w = nds {uyacw-ctp} (wind = no drop shot unless you are a championship world-class tennis player).

haiku 4

[beautiful girl]

she's riding her bicycle
super-fast hey beautiful
girl slow down

translated from numbers

[234444 49890]

0284234 03284 80-10
2390 65164 346 6661641
1340 08062 23

love. You and I and everyone belong somewhere and I belong here now for a few timeless days. We'll say that time has stopped as if it is our favorite room or a hidden clearing in a forest that

the tennis backhand

In the night, in the rain, the noises that allay the fears of being alone and lost are the noises that we grow tired of hearing during the day. When I first walked onto a tennis court I felt like I was lost in the night and in the rain but I couldn't allay my fears by listening to the noises I heard during the day because championship world-class tennis requires maximum focus and concentration.

(Everything else, including thought, should be blocked out of my human mind.)

My plan instead utilized subterfuge and camouflage but not the subterfuge and camouflage of vision or hearing. The subterfuge and camouflage of scent.

I thought that if I smelled like the places I felt lost in then no one would notice me. I wouldn't have to worry about being nervous while I was trying to find my way. Nobody would tell me that I held my tennis racquet the wrong way or that I needed to use my weak hand to control my two-handed backhand. It didn't even matter that the advice I was given about the two-handed backhand was true.

"One must find one's own way to one's own way."

--Bjorn McEnroe

There are other backhand styles also: the one-handed backhand with topspin and the one-handed backhand with slice. The flatter backhands. There is also the two-handed backhand with slice, which is rarely used but has been used on occasion to disquiet an unsuspecting opponent.

(Especially with my tennis backhand) the advice that I would give to amateurs is to remember that the backhand is the physical gesture (sporting or non-sporting) influenced by the human imagination more than any other physical gesture a human might make (including the physical gestures of play-acting). The tennis backhand has never been described objectively with everyday language and is, essentially, a fiction of the human mind—a creation, a phantom stroke that only appears to be real but is not (simply cannot) be real.

Champion's Note: to make yourself smell like the milieu of your fears so that you won't be nervous when you venture into strange places in which you are lost or feel lost:

1. Sweat before you enter the daunting milieu (i.e. bring your inner moisture(s) to your skin surface).

2. Open a new can of objects used in the daunting milieu and rub those objects all over the clothes that you've picked out to wear in the milieu. You can also rub the objects on your skin surface for longer lasting effect, thereby mixing it with your once inner moisture(s).

haiku 5

[sad family]

we are a sad family
who only talk about one thing
when we talk about everything

untranslated

never changes and in which we can pause without feeling that we have lost something we can never get back. So pause in this time as if all will return to the way it was before.

the tennis loss

Losing in tennis is the worst feeling in life. And a great loss is the greatest worst feeling in life ever. Yes, even I (a championship world-class tennis player) have felt loss's "ripping claws on my soul".

After a great loss I feel as though I can't travel the path of life set for me by the book (which, as "whatever gods if they exist are my witness", I will find again) that I found on that fateful day. I think about everything I did before my loss—as far back as I can remember. Was it because of the first word I ever spoke (murmur, murder, or water[i])?

Did I walk too late? Should I have played the piano instead of the trumpet? Or the oboe instead of the contrabassoon? What did I eat the year before? The month before? The day before? (Was it the broccoli?) Whose eye did I catch as I walked onto the tennis court? Did he or she remain in my subconscious to make me stumble at the most important moments. What could I have done? I remember the unremarkable happiness of the day before the great loss but:

"A great loss makes happiness irrelevant and exposes it for what it isn't: necessary for survival."

--Bjorn McEnroe

I have had many great victories but one great loss is equal to an infinity of great victories. And yet I hold on to time and the inhuman instinct to survive even when one feels like there is nothing left to live for (the arm wants to hit one more forehand, the hands to bake one more chocolate cake).

And without thinking about it I relive my great loss during all of the different units of time. I am overcome by grief at the millisecond of the second that I suffered my great loss, the second of the minute, the minute of the hour, the hour of the day, the day of the week, the week of the month, the month of the year, and if I were to live forever so on and so forth.

There are also microseconds, nanoseconds, picoseconds, etc. (and all the other unpredictable moments in time in which I am overcome by the grief of my great loss) even though they lie outside the bounds of temporal reasonableness for the human mind. But it can be said that within the most infinitesimal units of time I suffer my great loss and I suffer infinitely towards the emptiness of nothing.

My great loss was against the only tennis player who I had never beaten, who was objectively greater than I could ever have been, and who I loved more than any other tennis player I had ever played against. I have dreams about my great loss (68-70 in the final set) but I can't tell anyone about those dreams because they can't be explained with the language of the human mind.

(Final score of the great loss match: 0-6, 6-0, 0-6, 6-0, 68-70.)

haiku 6

[music from another room]

in love with other songs
the notes leave their measure

translated from the blank spaces between
the following words

[the perfume in your hair]

my arm is covered in skin
and reaches out to touch you

I've read that there is no before and no after and that time doesn't exist but I can't seem to live in a world where it doesn't exist. I've tried to think time away and be all of everyone that I am...I want to say

the tennis love

I met my real-world (non-tennis) love during the Baha Majoral Past Champion's tournament in downtown Tangier—the perfect setting for a small tournament of past champions who were not old but were old enough to be champions for many years. I was still young but tennis is a brutal sport for anyone who begins to decay (physically and morally) as I had begun to decay (I was only 29 in real life years but felt 34 or 35 in mental years).

My only goal when I was 29 was to find the book that started my foray into championship world-class tennis. I wasn't thinking about non-tennis (real-world) love at the time. Love in tennis means that you're losing. Love in the real (non-tennis) world means that you're winning.

It's the greatest irony of life that in tennis we run away from love because when other people (even those who play other sports or read tennis books) run towards love (perhaps with us) that we, who play championship world-class tennis, run away from love because we've trained all our lives to run away from love.

It takes years to forget the muscle memory (the arms muscle memory, the legs muscle memory, the hands muscle memory, but more importantly the brains muscle memory) that makes us eschew love.

As someone with a deftly soft touch on volleys I say that love is important and the only smidgeon of human DNA that has ensured the currently prolonged existence of humans on the only planet in the universe known (by we same humans) to have life. Tennis therefore is antithetical to human existence.

And yet I was struck by real-world love just as I had been struck by the tennis ball in "the tennis lob" chapter of these ruminations. Lelolah served the ball, so to speak, and I, for my part, decided not to return serve. I dropped my racquet and let the ball hit me roundly in my stomach where it has since remained embedded. We met at the net and (instead of shaking hands) we kissed. (We did not kiss. I stood next to her pretending to hit volleys with my racquet. "Love"ly Lelolah, who didn't play tennis, who danced, who still dances, and who I love more than I could ever pretend to.)

"As I write this book about championship world-class tennis I ponder if I should end every chapter with a quote by me or by someone else. In real life I've decided to end every conversation I have with an interesting, thought-provoking, and profound quote. It was difficult at first because I didn't realize how many conversations a person could have throughout the day—I spoke with people who worked at "stores", for example—and didn't always have a quote in my mind to end a conversation with so that sometimes I wouldn't speak or when someone started speaking to me I walked away as if I hadn't heard them. Therefore I put together a booklet of quotes to carry around with me, a sample of which I will include as an appendix herein, so that if you too undertake to end your conversations with interesting, thought-provoking, and profound quotes, you will have a variety of quote-grenades readily available. I call them quote-grenades because if anyone else is in hearing distance of the quote then they (the people within hearing distance) will also hear the quote and have their thoughts provoked."

--Bjorn McEnroe

"at the same time" and be everywhere I have ever been...also "at the same time", but I can't make this happen. I don't know if it's possible for me to exist without thinking that time

haiku 7

[genesis]

dead fish (scales?)
float to the surface shimmer
in first morning light

translated from english

[dawn]

deceased go fishing (balances?)
soar towards the superficial gleam
earliest original of dawn

also exists, whether it really exists or not. Maybe the illusion of time is a precondition for being one of the living and those who are no longer living are beyond time and have become

the tennis forehand

I made a direct appeal to my parents. My mother the woman who raised me and my father the man who raised me. They taught me to be freedom even if I wasn't free and to be love even if I wasn't loved. But they loved me. My appeal was a forehand blast down the line as my opponent came to the net. My parents didn't come to the net and they weren't my opponent but it was the only way I could think of appealing to them about the book I wanted to find. My father, who remembered the details of parties better than my mother did, said the party was at a friend's house. My mother said it was at my uncle's (her brother's) house. No, my father said.

--Your uncle was supposed to be at the party but it wasn't his house. I remember because Lelolah showed up.

--Lelolah? My Lelolah? She would have been my age. I thought I was the only—

--Not your Lelolah. There are other Lelolahs out there. That's why I remember. Nobody wanted her at the party because her boyfriend was Afro-Eurasian. That party. You remember (he looked at my mother). They said it was because he was a trouble maker and that he would show up if she was there but he never caused any trouble. We should have left the party right away. We left a little bit later. We told them to let her stay but she didn't want to stay after they started on her.

--I remember.   And you were in the basement bouncing a ball.   Every time the music stopped I heard it.   I was hoping no one else would hear it but I'm sure they did. And then I started listening for it in between songs (she smiled) as if you were speaking to me. I told your father we should have left with Lelolah.   We left only a few minutes after she did. We were trying to be nice and leave without being awkward. Imagine that. Lelolah was our friend and we let her down. I didn't see her much after that.   She probably thought we stayed at the party.

"Sometimes it's too late to do the right thing and it wouldn't change how people think about you and the people who you want to know about what you've done might never know what you did or wouldn't care because you did it too late and sometimes too late is like never but you should do it anyway."

--Bjorn McEnroe

--Is that why you held hands in the car on the way home that night?

My mother kissed my father on his forehead and touched his hand.

--We always hold hands my dear daughter (daughter?).

--Do you know where he lives now?

--Same house. He never moved. But we haven't spoken to him since.

The tennis forehand (especially mine) is the simplest and most effective way to dismantle an opponent. I didn't dismantle my parents but on the tennis court I've dismantled many (a.k.a. all) opponents with my tennis forehand. The tennis forehand should be struck with disinterested malice and aimed directly for the heart. To aim anywhere else is to leave an opponent merely wounded and invite divinely-begged-for vengeance.

As my parents spoke to each other the memories of the party came back to me as if they clicked the switch on an old movie projector that cast the images of that night onto the wall of their living room (if one took down the oil and acrylic painting of Buenos Aires): our arrival at the house, the crowded entrance hallway, the exaggerated guffaws, the disjointed conversations, the handshakes, the hugs, the hands tussling my hair, the lips kissing my cheeks, the smoke, the kitchen with food and bottles and glasses everywhere, the basement (quiet like a secret world except for the muffled music coming from above), the book underneath the sofa, the ball hitting the wall and bouncing on the tile floor, the woman's legs, the argument, and then the silence in the car and the lights of a city that must have seemed (that first time) like an alien landscape to me at such a late hour.

As their voices faded into the background, I heard the clicking of the projector mechanism in my head then music and the voice of a man I knew only as having one of the male singing voices of my childhood (starting quietly at first then increasing to normal decibel levels): "been down so long, getting up didn't cross my mind, I knew there was a better way of life that I was just trying to find. You don't know what you'll do until you're put under pressure. Across 110th street is a hell of a tester."

I was crossing 110th street and there was no turning back. I imagined hitting a tennis ball across the city (with my devastating forehand) that blasted into the house where the book was last seen, forming a charred chasm into a darkness I would enter and (after a long enough period of time that would make any on-lookers think "all was lost") exit triumphantly with the book in my hand.

The images from the party faded into the chromatic black Buenos Aires night and I turned to look at my parents who were still holding hands (and staring at me).

--Thanks Mom, Dad. I love you.

everything that ever was and ever will be. Even becoming indicates time. Do you remember what Maggie and I were talking about when we walked down into the basement?

haiku 8

[listen to me]

when I die I will leave
my records and record player
for my children

translated from light grey

[listen to me]

when I die I will leave
my records and record player
for my children

If you happened to
overhear us and if
you could guess
what we were
talking about maybe
it would help you
make everything
right again. I can't
tell you. You'll
have to see it for

the tennis serve

| BT | MEF | RLP | MER | IMP |

Early cocking   Middle cocking   Late cocking   Acceleration

The judges determine whether my serve is in or not. They also determine whether all my shots are in or not but the serve is the first shot they will make a judgement on during a point. If the serve is out I get to serve one more time (a second chance) and if I fail the second time there is no third chance and my opponent wins the point.

I had failed on my first serve in getting the book. It was a very hard, very flat (stretched-to-invisibly-thin flat) serve that bounced a few millimeters outside the corner of the service box (most likely an irregularity in my middle cocking): I introduced myself to the man who answered the door and asked him if he remembered the party; if he remembered a book he kept in the basement that perhaps he had lost and perhaps had been looking for but couldn't find until the day after the party when he was tidying up and found it on the top of the stairs (where I left it). I was the kid in the basement, son of etc. etc., who were friends with etc., etc.

--I remember it.

--Do you still have it?

--I do.

--Is it possible that I can buy it from you?

--Nope. I broke my leg because of that book. I slipped on it when I was going down the stairs into the basement that day. No hard feelings son. But it's part of my basement book collection of books now. I hated that book. Thought to burn it or shred it but I spent a couple of months immobile and recovering on my living room sofa and decided hate was no way to be living and in a strange way the book taught me that. I mean, like I'm going to say very soon "never read it" (he raised his hands and made quote marks in the air starting with the word "never" and lowered his hands after the word "it").

--Can you tell me what it's called?

--The man who walked slow with a gun and wrote poems.

--The man who walked with a gun and wrote poems.

--Slow with a gun.

--Slow with a gun and wrote. What's it about?

--Don't know. Never read it.

--Do you think I can borrow it?

--I don't think so. Look, there are important things, really important things going on in the world today and all you care about is getting your hands on a book? My book, by the way. Why don't you go buy yourself a copy? Also, I have a march to go to with my wife today.

--A march?

--Yes, a march. If you care about the world and the people oppressed by a greedy bunch of fuckwits then you should march too. We'll be marching all day.

--I do care. I care about people.

--Why do you want the book anyway?

There are many types of serves that can be used to win a point. I tried the hard, flat serve to ace my opponent and win the point instantaneously but it didn't work. There is also the spin serve that bounces away from the opponent. It's a slower, safer serve but it's less direct and trickier. If an opponent should get on top of it, however, the point would also be over instantaneously (in their favor). But I couldn't risk missing another hard and flat serve.

--It's not that important. Just trying to tie up some loose memory ends. I'm reflecting on my life and for some reason I have a very clear memory of that book. I was just in the neighborhood.

I couldn't tell him that it was the book that started me on my destiny to being a championship world-class tennis player. The words were in my brain but they never made their way to my vocal chords and out through my mouth. I didn't lie though. I really was trying to tie up some loose memory ends.

(Without thinking I might have voiced an asemic phrase[ii] that I scratched with my racquet on center court during a match against Bolo Li before the final point of the final game of the final set of the final match of the Aunt and Uncle Brasilia Open Championships.)

I felt a strange satisfaction—not strange in the way the satisfaction felt but strange in the reason that I felt the satisfaction— knowing that the book also helped someone else. I felt that it was my book because it helped me first (with my destiny) and then helped someone else (the day after when he slipped on it and broke his leg and then in the following weeks and months when he was immobile on his living room sofa and decided that hate was no way to be living).

I hurried to meet Lelolah (my) and tell her about the slow spin serve I was going to hit and ask her if she wanted to be my doubles partner and do some hitting with me. All we had to do was break the lock on the back door of the house or find an unopened window (preferred method), tip-toe around the house to find the book, and then leave as if we were leaving quietly. If she didn't want to hit with me then I would hit by myself or ask my *ami en guerre* DJ Titan T-Rex to hit with me. I knew Lelolah better than anyone else in the world ever knew Lelolah but I still couldn't tell you what she would do. She was so mysterious.

yourself or you'll
never see it.   It
can't be described.
If I try to describe
it I think it would
only confuse you
more.   I can only
help you by saying
that if your eyes
can't see it then
the problem is with

haiku 9

[at night, remember, it's love everybody]

a little drunk you take
my hand we run to the bus
already driving away

translated from photograph

your eyes and not
with the thing that
you are trying to
see.   Think.   I will
be back to write
more soon.   I am
baking a chocolate
cake for your
parents who want
me to taste their
favorite white rose

the tennis interview

In the past I was shy about speaking to strangers; but having conversations with the strangers in my life has become less fretful (since I've created my booklet of quotes). I don't know the average number of strangers a person has in his or her life but I think the number of strangers that I've had in my life has been above average (because of my renown).

Sometimes I spoke to my strangers several times a week. I even spoke to one of my strangers twice during the same day (I presented him with two quotes—one I thought more profound than the other with the imbalance of the divergent levels of profundity vexing me until I spoke to him two days later to restore the balance with another slightly less profound quote so that the two slightly less profound quotes were equal to the more profound quote).

I recently spoke to one of the strangers in my life named Florentina who is still the classy and famous host of the television show The Tennis Life in Retrospect.

Florentina: So Mr. Bjorn McEnroe, or Bjornie Mac as you're known to your fans, you're no longer playing championship world-class tennis but we've heard you're working on a documentary about your tennis life.

Bjorn McEnroe: Not a documentary Florentina (I used my stranger's name).   A book. It's really about helping other people grow in their tennis life. I sprinkle in tropical anecdotes regarding my upbringing and my human development. I also write about my parents.

Florentina: Is it finished or are you still writing it?

Bjorn McEnroe: It's finished Florentina. I finished writing it last week.

Florentina: Is there anything from the book that you can tell us that we don't already know about your tennis life that hasn't unfolded before our very eyes since you were a youngster? Anything about the dramatis personae (I deduced the meaning) that have played a supporting role?

It was at this moment of the interview that I leaned back in my chair and crossed my legs (in the European style). I looked at Lelolah who was seated on a chair behind

Florentina, in the dimness of the unlit corner of the room behind the television camera and the bright lights that shined down on Florentina and me. Lelolah. My Lelolah. And me. Bjorn McEnroe. Her Bjorn McEnroe.

I could imagine that I was gazing upon her from the universe as she sat on the chair with her legs crossed in the ceiling-less room and materializing only when a faraway diffusion of light reached the boundaries of her elegantly formed human frame and brought the silhouette of her body into being before the light faded and she (and the way that I saw her) along with it.

Bjorn McEnroe: Frankly Florentina, it isn't what's in the book that matters. Books have been helping people since the beginning of time. And no one can be sure people actually read them. There's no scientific evidence that people read the books they say they read and no scientific proof that what's inside a book is of any consequence to a person's life. Also, and this is important, I just don't think so. You don't have to read a book for it to have influence in your life.

Florentina: What books have had an influence in your life whether you have read them or not?

I knew that Lelolah was looking at me but I suddenly felt that she was looking at me in such a way that I could turn to you or any of the other strangers in my life and say that "I felt her looking at me".

Bjorn McEnroe: Not books Florentina (the sound of my voice became a whisper). Book. The man who walked slow with a gun and wrote poems (the sentence trailed off so that the words "and wrote poems" were almost inaudible).

I felt Lelolah get up from her chair. I felt the door to the room open and close. I didn't have to look up to know that she was gone.

haiku 10

[night]

the lateness of the hour
expands and all is being
undertaken

[translated from cricket chirp]

tea they drink with a little honey. Do you bake for them? I'm back and I want to tell you that you should bake for your parents. You don't have to bake chocolate cake. You can start with muffins. I'm not

the tennis trick shot

I had taken great care to place my foot between (what I recognized as) rows of daffodils—*narcissus hispanicus and angel's tears*—growing beneath the kitchen window and had even lightened my body pressure to such an extent that I would not disturb the dirt I pressed upon as I climbed through the barely large enough opening.

But somewhere during my climb, the technique of my climbing motion went awry, I lost track of my right foot (faulty proprioception under stress leading to the most consequential foot fault of my life), and squashed some flowers. I could only hope the damage I had done could be undone with a little tender love and care. I asked Titan to make sure he caused no more damage to the daffodils (I used the scientific term) as he followed me in.

The house was quiet as one might expect, as if it were sleeping, and would only awaken once the people who lived there returned. I felt foolish for having brought my inner moisture(s) to the surface before we broke in because I felt like I belonged there, after all.

Titan and I moved quickly through the rooms until we found the stairs to the basement. The house was smaller than I remembered and the basement even more so but I was a smaller person (a child with a boy body and boy brain) the last time I was there. I observed many likeable objects in the house (a pencil, a record player, a green blanket, a framed photograph of a woman who might be mistaken for a fondly remembered school teacher) and I surmised that the house was a place where the person or persons who lived there could be happy even if they could be happy nowhere else in the world. In the basement there were two bookshelves filled with hundreds of books. Titan searched through one of them while I searched through the other.

"I don't often comment on bookshelves but a bookshelf with only twenty or thirty books and some empty space is more captivating than a bookshelf filled to capacity with hundreds of books. It's also easier to find the book you're looking for."

--Bjorn McEnroe

--I found it.

I heard the three words "echo in my mind". This was the moment I had been waiting for since my championship world-class tennis career ended. In the moment of my choosing I would turn to Titan and see the book that started—nay, propelled me on my destiny. In my mind I heard a tennis umpire speak through his microphone to the throng of spectators applauding me (also in my mind): "quiet please". And all became quiet for the briefest of moments. Until Titan's voice.

--Aren't you going to look at it?

I was hoping for more quiet but I heard the words he spoke at the most miniscule vibration unit of the stratified squamous epithelium of his vocal cords. In fact, my senses had become so attuned to the universe and all of humanity therein that I heard the disturbance of the air around his arm (and possibly the disturbance of the air around that air) as he reached out to hand me my prize—like so many others had done after my many great tennis victories. But this victory was even more great! So great, in fact, that I felt I loved the world (again) and all of the people (just the good people) who lived in it. I put my arm out to stop him (without looking).

--Not yet. I'm thinking.

I was thinking that Lelolah should have been there with me—and then I heard voices from upstairs. Titan and I turned to each other (one could say in a panic). I tried to look away from the book in Titan's hand but when he and I ducked behind the sofa to hide from whomever we heard in the room(s) above us I caught a glimpse of the book's shape and I knew, like one man striking another man with a nearby tire iron, that whatever book Titan was holding was not the book I was searching for.

The situation reminded me of a match I played in Oolong Province in which I hit a stunning overhead only to have my opponent run up along the stadium wall behind, jump up in the air when he reached the top of the wall, then hit the ball between his legs and beyond my reach before he landed. Tennis players rarely hit trick shots and when they do, they usually do so—despite the spectacular nature of the trick shot—out of hopelessness because the trick shot seldom results in a winning point.

As I curled up behind the sofa in the basement of the house on that street in that small town of that sparsely populated county I felt the same way I felt when I was the victim of that tennis trick shot in Oolong Province so many years ago. I looked at the book's title: The Man Who Walked Slow With A Gun and Wrote Poems. The title was correct (or?) but the book was a small paperback. It wasn't humanly possible to hit a tennis ball against any wall with such a teensy-weensy book. I compared myself to the squashed daffodils. Only instead of me squashing the daffodils (and myself), somebody or something else (perhaps another destiny) squashed them, and in squashing them, squashed me too.

asking you to
become a baker.
I'm asking you to
pretend to be
something other
than what you are
pretending to be
right now because I
love you but I
don't like what you
are pretending to

haiku 11

[riding on the train]

i don't always know

what's happening in a book

i read over someone's shoulder

[translated from the mirror]

i don't always know

what's happening in a book

i read over someone's shoulder

be. Maybe we are all pretending but at least we can pretend to be good people. At least that. And then maybe we will become what we pretend to be. I've seen it happen to other people. It

the tennis volley

Fig. 1

If the basement had become that state between sleep and wakefulness (hypnagogia) then the rooms above us had become a dream. I thought I heard Lelolah's voice and (without thinking) started humming a song that Lelolah and I danced to after dinner (and sometimes before). I imagined her dancing upstairs, alone in the dark, dreary world (hearing the hazy intonations of our song but never knowing that it was I who intoned) and I was overcome by a feeling of sadness.

(And then within the first imagining I imagined Lelolah looking at herself in a mirror, combing her long hair, while silence marched on her from all sides like an invading army, destroying our song's melody—note by note, measure by measure—as it closed in.)

"If not the imagining then the imagining within the imagining."

--Bjorn McEnroe

Was I overcome with a feeling of sadness because I imagined Lelolah all alone in the dark, dreary world up there or because the book that was within my grasp had turned out to be the book I shouldn't be grasping?

I peeked over the sofa but Titan pulled me back down and held my face against the floor (shushing me even though I didn't need to be shushed). And there underneath the sofa—the only place my vision could take me at that precise moment in the history of time—I saw the shape of a wide, flat object.

--Darling, are you down there?

Lelolah.

--Titan, are you down there too?

Margaret.

Lelolah wasn't alone, after all (though the world still seemed dark and dreary). I reached my arm underneath the sofa just as I had done when I was a boy and slowly pulled the object out as if it were the last, loose tooth in a mouth that no longer needed teeth.

--Do we need it though?

--I wouldn't say we need it and maybe that's its primary characteristic. It's an autonomous and self-contained thing, untethered from everything else.

--Actually Lelo, the way you explain it maybe it's even beyond necessity.

--I like that Maggie. Yes, beyond necessity. There can't even be necessity without it. It's like life itself.

--It all seems so circular Lelo but it's nice to think about.

The object I found underneath the sofa was a book titled *13 Haiku by Various Artists (with Illustrations).* I knew in my heart and soul (if humans had hearts and souls) that this was the book I used to hit the tennis ball against the wall of that very basement. As a championship world-class tennis player it would have been enough for me to convince any doubters simply by saying "I could feel it in my hands".

But I felt disappointment in my tennis being because I just couldn't imagine telling the world that a book of haiku "started— nay, propelled me on my destiny". I stood up and placed the book of haiku on one side of the sofa and placed the book I took from Titan on the other side of the sofa. The two books faced each other across the line that separated the two worn-out but well-kept sofa cushions: *The Man Who Walked Slow With a Gun and Wrote Poems* vs. *13 Haiku by Various Artists (with Illustrations).*

The two books were like two tennis players firing volley after volley across the net from each other until at last the ball flew off the edge of one player's racquet and against the chain link fence of Stoney Brook Public Tennis Court #1.

Champion's Note: the best way to describe the technique of hitting a good volley is to pretend that your tennis racquet is your hand and that you are trying to catch the ball with your tennis racquet.

The Man Who Walked Slow With a Gun and Wrote Poems had a better title, probably with an edgy story to match.

13 Haiku by Various Artists (with Illustrations) was a book of haiku with drawings.

The Man Who Walked Slow With a Gun and Wrote Poems had guns in it and readers liked stories with guns.

The title *13 Haiku by Various Artists (with Illustrations)* was uninspiring and evoked no images or feelings which (if I remembered from my elementary school days) is what haiku are supposed to do.

The Man Who Walked Slow With a Gun and Wrote Poems probably had tough characters (guns) who weren't afraid to show their softer side (poems) and readers loved those types of characters. It probably had all the other good characters that readers loved too (or at least recognized): characters who were certain of themselves and of their place in the world; who lived with conviction; who redeemed themselves; who were professional honchos or amateur kingpins and made others think there was something unique about them; who inspired readers (to do things?).

Even though *The Man Who Walked Slow With a Gun and Wrote Poems* wasn't the book that started my foray into championship world-class tennis, it was a book that fit with the image I had of myself and with the story of my life that I wanted to tell to inspire others. It would also allow me to be a better influence on children because children would listen to me if I told them that I was inspired by an edgy book like *The Man Who Walked Slow With a Gun and Wrote Poems.*

The two books went back and forth until the ball clanged off the racquet of *13 Haiku by Various Artists (with Illustrations)* and into the net. *The Man Who Walked Slow With a Gun and Wrote Poems* had won. I cheered but noticed that Lelolah didn't cheer (Titan and Margaret didn't cheer either).

I would tell the world that *The Man Who Walked Slow With a Gun and Wrote Poems* was the book that started me on my destiny. I didn't consider it a lie in the same way that Lelolah did. I explained (or tried to explain) to her that I was keeping a secret: something sacred I wanted to hold onto for myself (it was my life, after all), like a clean, white, cozy blanket that I slept with and that I didn't want sullied by the touch of too many human hands. I also wanted to be a good influence on children.

haiku 12

[going away]

a plane flies over

our motel room the ceiling plaster

unpeels dust onto our bed

[translated from traditional 5-7-5 haiku]

airplane flies over

our motel room the ceiling

dust falls on our bed

can happen to us
too. We can even
pretend that the
world isn't always a
dark and dreary
place. We can play
this game like we
play tennis and we
might even be able
to win. So think.
Remember that I

the tennis overhead

I sat in the garden, among the flowers and flying insects, stirring the bright sunlight floating in my cup of tea when I saw in the kitchen window the reflection of a bluebird flying toward the great firmament (in my suffering it was no longer the sky) and I thought about how the bluebird was just like Lelolah fluttering away from our cozy little house with her beautiful blue wings and orange-ish belly. Even in her departure Lelolah was still beautiful. I wondered when I would see her again (I begged to "whatever gods if they existed" to give me one more chance). I looked up to the great firmament to see if the bluebird gave any indication that it would fly back but I saw nothing—not even the slightest feathery innuendo of return.

I should have told Florentina and the whole world the truth about the book that started my foray into championship world-class tennis (*13 Haiku by Various Artists (with Illustrations)*). I thought about how disappointed my parents would be if they knew about what I had done. I wondered if Lelolah hadn't already told them or if they hadn't already seen my tennis interview.

A breeze blew over me. Not the usual innocent breeze that brought with it that illusion of freedom that at times made life so sweet. My lie (and—double shame—theft, because I stole both books) attracted a sinister breeze that had never blown over me before, that covered me with the soot of my own deceitfulness, and filled up all the creases of my lying face and body with a creepy darkness so that I no longer looked like a human being but only the crudest sketch of a human being.

In tennis terms I would say that I only needed to hit a simple overhead (tell the truth) to win the point but I flubbed it. The overhead is the most difficult tennis shot for amateurs to hit but for championship world-class tennis players it is the easiest of shots that is rarely, if ever, flubbed. I knew I had to hit another overhead (against myself) to make everything right with Lelolah, my parents, and the world again. I drank my tea (it was too tasty to leave to the insects) and went back inside to rework my how-to-play-tennis manuscript.

In my book I would tell the truth about the book that started my foray into championship world-class tennis and hope that Lelolah, my parents, and the rest of the world forgave me. I even thought about having haiku Sundays (or Saturdays—either day would be good) at our house and invite my friends over for breakfast to write and recite haiku with Lelolah and me. We could still play tennis during the afternoon and drink at night. I sent the edited manuscript to Lelolah (she was staying with my parents—who still thought I was their daughter) and waited for her to respond.

When she finally responded (three agonizing days later) she wrote that she and Margaret had decided to play singles for a little while (what did Titan do?) and that she still loved me but was going to stay with my parents for another few weeks to draw pictures for my new book without being disturbed by me, by the complications of tennis, or by the whole world (except for my parents and Margaret).

"The trees, the leaves falling from the trees, the dry grass of a desolate field, the horses that sometimes run there, the history of my time here, the horses will be gone before me and I will be gone before the trees, then time will be gone and nothing will exist."

--Bjorn McEnroe

will return. How will you be when I return? What will your face look like? Will your body move with grace and beauty? With the grace of that which exists beyond necessity or the clumsy gesticulations

haiku 13

[purgatory]

overcome by deep
sadness the devil himself
takes pity on me

[translated from despair]

of someone of an ugly character. But think. Because I don't always know what I'm talking about. Who does? I'm searching just like you are. Talk soon yeah?

Love,
Lelolah

the tennis book booklet of quotes

- -
(cut here then bind)

"I have no talent. And therefore, I must make do with a common, mediocre soul. And to admit with the little sincerity I have and without pretension, that I desire a simple life and that I am profoundly happy with the little things that I have and with my place in the universe."

--S{E}AN?

"We are but foot soldiers in the march of our blood."

--Phillipa Panshi

"There is a relationship between music and flying that has yet to be studied. For example, how the arc of a crow's flight influences the texture of a Beethoven sonata. Or how the delicate shifts of a pigeon's wing effects cadence in a Mahler symphony or a Janacek concerto."

--Ludwig Van Brijbasi

"Small things are the loose thread of the pallbearer's shoe. The pallbearer's shoe is a well-travelled instrument of the foot."

--Mergon Droodle

"The pebbles on the bank of the river are covered then uncovered by water. A cold and simple action that is but the last link of a long, unseen chain."

--Ortwright Gerder

"It was a certain kind of paradise if only one could forget where one was."

--Annaphasia McGergersson

"E. and I cuddle our life with our minds and our hearts. But we are like the detritus of unmindful pockets and the pebbles on the thoroughfare. We land where we are dropped and we go where we are kicked."

--S.

"We think that one day we will understand. Not because we are thoughtful or inspired but because the reason will simply become clear to us. And we'll come to understand that this reason is not so important, after all."

--Thor Ruiz

"Only those who made me could have made me, and only at a particular moment in history, and if not then, then never."

--Carmen Mériméé

"One of the reasons I live here is because of the floor. It took me years to find a room with this type of floor."

--Paul Eugene Paul

"…it is peculiar that someone mistook me for a dolphin, because there really is no resemblance (other than the glossy, wet look of my skin). I don't like swimming, unless the water is deep—ocean deep, and even then it's only the sensation of floating from bottom to top that I relish. The act of swimming itself never appealed to me."

--Vladimira (Mira) Oblonsky

"I don't have coherent thoughts. I try my best."

--S{E}AN?

"It tells us that regardless of any radical characterization or plot, the human mind is incapable of thinking beyond the same flimsy skin and limp spine it has grown accustomed to. Greatness is what it always has been. But we know this isn't true. Or so we hope."

--Lelolah (at 23)

"It was a hollow feeling because it made me realize that sometimes when I think the world is coming to an end it really isn't."

--Lelolah (at 24)

"Where do we belong? Where do we come from? Why are we here?"

--Lelolah (at 24 ½)

[i] murmur (from Stories for Nadira)

Contained in this matter and also within the container of this matter is the idea that the first word spoken by me when scientifically I was of conscious mind but practically of none are the arguments or observations set forth below (arguments or observations—they are set forth below).

My mother and father would say to other people that the first word I ever spoke that was not an evocation of the simple coo or a guttural attempt at replication of a random sound heard 'round me was: "murder".

No, it couldn't be. Are you sure? And with absolute certainty my mother (not so much my father) would say absolutely.

Couldn't it be "mudder" or something similar sounding as to be close to "mother", which although unusual for a child's first word, probably wasn't unheard of, and certainly presented better than "murder" to friends and family?

"No, it was *murder*. I was (and still am) a big fan of violent crime and any time I had trouble with any task or my day was going badly I would say to anyone within earshot of me that this or that was "murder". The person who spent the most time within earshot of me was my baby boy. Not that I would murder anyone. Obviously my pronouncements were more nounial than verbial if I can be allowed to speak those words for the first time as if I am also of scientific but not practical consciousness."

However, my father's refined uncertainty (and unrefined certainty, as he revealed to me one night in drunken amusement that he was sure my first word was "murmur"—a word whose (?) beauty he argued had never faded but had perhaps become undervalued by the reading and listening public) led me to believe that my first word might have been another.

At different times in my life I hoped my first word was "Paris" in honor of the rooftops there where one might gaze over mist-covered enclaves and behind their assemblage the soft glow of a sun that looks upon all the world's cities (mostly) alike but stares at this one (sometimes inappropriately). Or perhaps "Lelolah" after the woman whose many friends and lovers killed themselves and who, in the end, killed herself too. Or "pantomime". A word I could never have known and that I have never heard my mother or father say and is ("to be honest") a word rarely found in anyone's lexicon.

My brother who is seven years older than I am, however, told me that he heard me say "water" the day after I was born. He never told anyone because he thought no one would believe him. But he was absolutely certain ("ain't no doubt") that the day after I was born I held on tightly to his thumb with my *très petit* new-born-baby fingers, looked him straight in his eyes and, without a tremble in my voice, said "water". He thought I was thirsty but wasn't sure if water was something I should be drinking.

So: murder, murmur, or water. One of these is the first word I ever spoke.

ii 𝕵𝖖𝖇